Dear Parents:

Congratulations! Your child is taking the first steps on an exciting journey. The destination? Independent reading!

STEP INTO READING® will help your child get there. The program offers five steps to reading success. Each step includes fun stories and colorful art or photographs. In addition to original fiction and books with favorite characters, there are Step into Reading Non-Fiction Readers, Phonics Readers and Boxed Sets, Sticker Readers, and Comic Readers—a complete literacy program with something to interest every child.

Learning to Read, Step by Step!

Ready to Read   Preschool–Kindergarten
• big type and easy words • rhyme and rhythm • picture clues
For children who know the alphabet and are eager to begin reading.

Reading with Help   Preschool–Grade 1
• basic vocabulary • short sentences • simple stories
For children who recognize familiar words and sound out new words with help.

Reading on Your Own   Grades 1–3
• engaging characters • easy-to-follow plots • popular topics
For children who are ready to read on their own.

Reading Paragraphs   Grades 2–3
• challenging vocabulary • short paragraphs • exciting stories
For newly independent readers who read simple sentences with confidence.

Ready for Chapters   Grades 2–4
• chapters • longer paragraphs • full-color art
For children who want to take the plunge into chapter books but still like colorful pictures.

STEP INTO READING® is designed to give every child a successful reading experience. The grade levels are only guides; children will progress through the steps at their own speed, developing confidence in their reading.

Remember, a lifetime love of reading starts with a single step!

For Freddy—my fierce nephew!
—D.R.S.

Published in the United States by Random House Children's Books, a division of Penguin Random House LLC, 1745 Broadway, New York, NY 10019, and in Canada by Penguin Random House Canada Limited, Toronto. Step into Reading, Random House, and the Random House colophon are registered trademarks of Penguin Random House LLC.
Visit us on the Web!
StepIntoReading.com
rhcbooks.com
Educators and librarians, for a variety of teaching tools, visit us at RHTeachersLibrarians.com
ISBN 978-0-593-37303-3 (trade) — ISBN 978-0-593-37304-0 (lib. bdg.) —
ISBN 978-0-593-37305-7 (ebook)
Printed in the United States of America
10 9 8 7 6 5 4 3
Random House Children's Books supports the First Amendment and celebrates the right to read.

STEP 3 STEP INTO READING®
READING ON YOUR OWN

DINOSAURS in the WILD!

by Dennis R. Shealy

Random House New York

The Jurassic World dinosaurs

have escaped . . .

into our world!

Now a *T. rex* roams the streets. . . .

Flying reptiles, such as

Quetzalcoatluses

and *Pteranodons,*

soar through the skies. . . .

And giant swimming reptiles,
including *Mosasaurus,*
lurk in the ocean depths.
Now that they live among us,
let's get to know some of these
amazing creatures.

Tyrannosaurus rex—T. rex—
is a ferocious predator.
She is always ready to defend
her territory and her title
as the greatest carnivore
of all time!

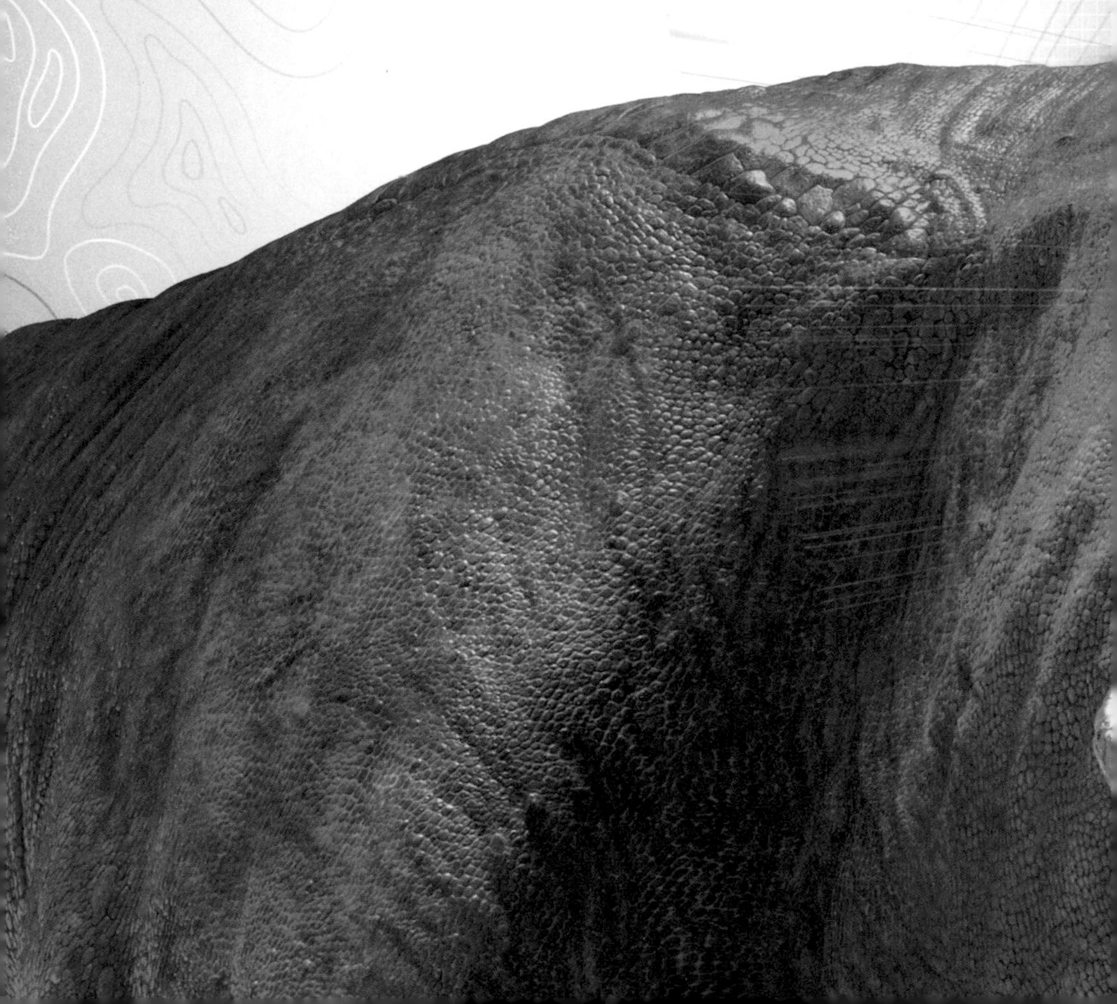

The *T. rex* has some competition
from the *Giganotosaurus.*
This dinosaur is bigger
than the *T. rex* and equally fierce.

If these two formidable predators ever fight, the battle will be a rip-roaring epic!

Other big meat eaters
to keep an eye out for are
Baryonyx, Allosaurus,
and *Carnotaurus.*

All three of these dinosaurs
have powerful jaws and
sharp teeth
that can crush any prey.

Smaller, but no less fierce,
are Blue and Beta.
These two *Velociraptors*
are swift predators
with sharp, sickle-shaped claws
on each foot.
They are quickly learning
to survive in a vast
mountain wilderness.

Pyroraptor is covered
in bright fiery-red feathers.

Like other raptors, she is
a quick, quiet hunter.
Pyroraptor has traveled
to many places—
from dark, dense jungles
to cold, snowy mountains.

Like the *Velociraptors* but larger, *Atrociraptors* are aggressive hunters.

Panthera, Red, Ghost, and Tiger are four *Atrociraptors* that have been trained to hunt humans!

Dinosaurs come in other sizes and stranger shapes, too. The small *Dilophosaurus* has a wide, colorful neck frill that she can open to scare her enemies away. She can also spit a deadly black venom with lethal accuracy!

The *Parasaurolophus* has
a long crest on her head.
This large but gentle
plant eater
uses the crest to make
loud bellowing sounds
to communicate with
her herd.

Named after an Aztec serpent god, the *Quetzalcoatlus* is one of the largest flying animals ever.

She is related to the *Pteranodon*, and her sharp, toothless beak is a powerful weapon.

The huge *Therizinosaurus*
has long, powerful claws—
but they are for slicing
and shredding leaves.
This feathered dinosaur
only eats plants!

The *Dimetrodon* is crocodile-like
with a large spiny fin
on her back.
She has a mouth full of cone-shaped
teeth that are perfect for grabbing
slippery frogs and fish
to eat.

BELIEVE IT OR NOT, THE
DIMETRODON
IS MORE CLOSELY RELATED
TO MAMMALS
THAN TO REPTILES OR
DINOSAURS!

Jurassic World dinosaurs come in so many shapes and sizes.
They are spreading around the globe, looking for new habitats to fill.

Whether they hunt animals
or eat plants and insects,
they will find a way
to survive.

Show the Jurassic World dinosaurs respect, because one day they may hold dominion over the whole earth!